Library of Congress Cataloging in Publication Data: Lionni, Leo, 1910-   A flea story: I want to
stay here! I want to go there! SUMMARY: Two fleas, one who loves to travel and one who prefers
staying home, decide to go their separate ways. [1. Fleas—Fiction] I. Title. PZ7.L66341ak [E]
77-4322 ISBN 0-394-83498-4 ISBN 0-394-93498-9 lib. bdg.

A Flea Story
by Leo Lionni

Pantheon

We have been here much too long. Aren't you ever curious about the rest of the world? Just think—we have never seen the ear. I want to go there.
It is soft and warm. I am perfectly happy. I have no desire to jump about. I want to stay here.

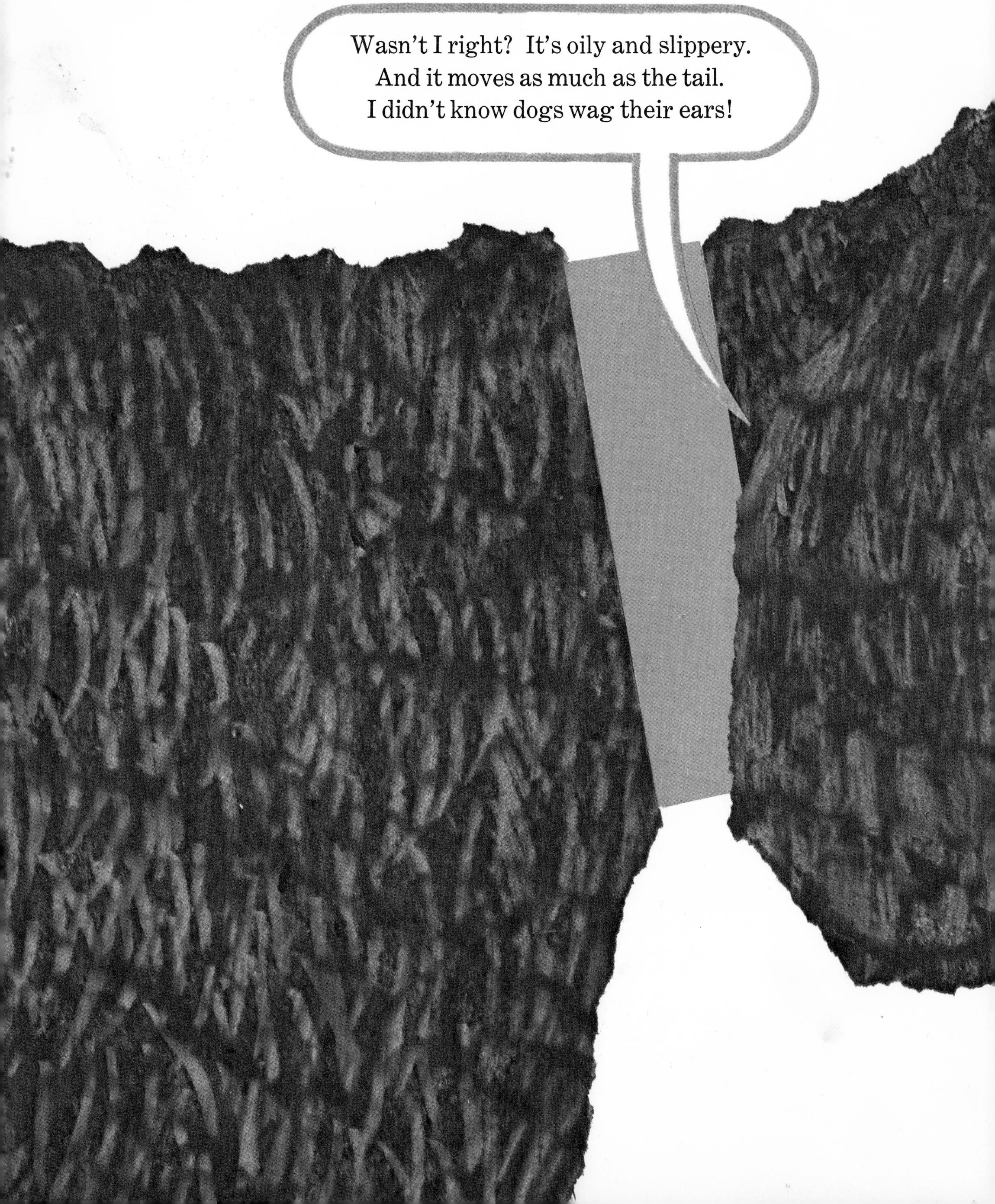
Wasn't I right? It's oily and slippery. And it moves as much as the tail. I didn't know dogs wag their ears!

You have no sense of beauty.
The skin is smooth. And
there is a tunnel, round
and mysterious.

Everything here is hard and cold. The quills are like a forest in winter. Please let's go back to the dog.
Oh, you and your dog! Don't you enjoy traveling and seeing new things? Look! In that hole there is a mole!

Don't tell me the mole isn't soft and warm. And how exciting to be inside the earth!
I'm afraid in the dark and you know it!

Look where the turtle has taken us. A duck! Now we can travel on the water. Perhaps she'll take us to Africa or Australia!
I am tired of struggling with you. This, I assure you, will be my last adventure.

Well rejoice! You won't have to be seasick. Here is our chance to fly.
I will do nothing of the kind. I have followed you on the strangest animals, inside the earth and on the water. Here is where I put my foot down!

It is extraordinary! From here everything is almost as small as we are. A cow is no bigger than a bumblebee, and the woods are like flocks of sheep, huddled together in meadows. Someday I'll come back and tell you all about it. But will words be enough?

I smell something familiar.
How long have I been away from
the dog? Another few hops
and I'll be home.

Finally! It is good to be in soft, warm fur once more. It is a little lonely now, but when we are together again, between what I have seen and what I will be told, I shall know something about the world. And, who knows, now and then I may want to travel a bit.